DISCARD

A NEW HOME

Mexico
City

New York City

A NEW HOME

Tania de Regil

CANDLEWICK PRESS

Mom and Dad told me that we
are moving to Mexico City.

Mamá and Papá told me that we are moving to New York City.

But I'm not sure I want to leave my home

because I'm going to miss lots of things.

Like listening to my favorite song on
my way to school in the morning.

And getting something delicious to eat
on my way home in the afternoon.

Cheering loudly for our team

to win at the stadium.

And spending nights out watching

the dancers at the concert hall.

But what if there is nowhere for

me to play in my new city?

Or no places for my class

to explore our past?

I know my home can be hard on some people.

And sometimes it can be very noisy.

But I'll miss all the fun we have

around the city in the summer.

And I'll also miss

playing with my friends.

I hope my life won't be so

different in my new city.

I really hope I like

my new home.

Here is some
information about
the two amazing
cities featured
in this book!

NEW YORK CITY has been welcoming immigrants since it was founded nearly four hundred years ago. People from all across the globe have come to call it their home, making it one of the most diverse cities in the world.

CIUDAD DE MÉXICO (Mexico City) is the oldest capital in the Americas. Its origins go back nearly 700 years to the Aztecs, who found their promised land on a small island in the middle of a lake.

The MUSIC OF NEW YORK CITY is as plentiful and diverse as its people, and there's no better place to showcase it than in the NYC subway. Musicians audition every year for a spot in the Music Under New York program.

Out of all the different types of MEXICO CITY'S STREET MUSIC, the street organ stands out for its nostalgic tunes. Organists, known as cilindreros, dress in the traditional uniform worn by soldiers during the Mexican Revolution.

HOT DOGS are a classic American food, but their origin is due in large part to a German immigrant who, in 1871, opened a hot dog stand on Coney Island, where it quickly became a fast food standard.

ELOTES (corn on the cob) and ESQUITES (corn kernels served in a cup) are delicious traditional Mexican snacks. They are usually topped with mayonnaise, lime juice, crumbly cheese, salt, and chili powder.

YANKEE STADIUM is home to the Yankees, who have won twenty-seven World Series Championships. Many of baseball's most famous players have donned the pin-striped uniform, including Mickey Mantle, Babe Ruth, Joe DiMaggio, and Lou Gehrig.

ESTADIO AZTECA (Aztec Stadium) in Mexico City is regarded as one of the most iconic soccer stadiums in the world. It has hosted two FIFA World Cup finals, in 1970 and 1986, making stars out of Pelé and Maradona.

LINCOLN CENTER is home to thirty performance spaces that showcase a wonderful array of performing arts, such as the New York City Ballet. Its first audience included the construction workers who built the theater, along with their families.

The PALACIO DE BELLAS ARTES (Palace of Fine Arts) has hosted some of Mexico's most important cultural events. It's well known for its many murals and its stained-glass stage curtain, which was assembled in New York by Tiffany & Company.

CENTRAL PARK is the most visited park in the United States and the most filmed park in the world. Construction began in 1857 and continued even through the Civil War. It was finally completed in 1873.

BOSQUE DE CHAPULTEPEC (Chapultepec Forest) is one of the largest city parks in the Western Hemisphere. In the heart of the park is the only royal castle in North America, Castillo de Chapultepec (Chapultepec Castle).

The AMERICAN MUSEUM OF NATURAL HISTORY houses the largest collection of fossil mammals and dinosaurs in the world, including one of the largest carnivorous dinosaurs ever found — the tyrant king of lizards, *Tyrannosaurus rex.*

The MUSEO NACIONAL DE ANTROPOLOGÍA (National Museum of Anthropology) is home to many of Mexico's archaeological wonders, including the Sun Stone, which was found buried below the Zócalo (central square) in 1790.

HOMELESSNESS in New York City has reached the highest levels since the Great Depression of the 1930s. Unfortunately, the cost of living has become so expensive over the past few years that people have been forced to leave their homes, causing thousands to sleep on the streets.

Mexico's extreme WEALTH INEQUALITY results in thousands of people from across the country going to the capital in search of a better life. Sadly, many end up living in extreme poverty, forced to live and work on the streets.

TIMES SQUARE is one of the world's busiest pedestrian areas. With thousands of tourists visiting the area every day, foot traffic has become as much of an issue as automobile traffic.

THE ANILLO PERIFÉRICO (peripheral ring) that encircles Mexico City serves as the main road that allows the city's heavy traffic to flow.

CONEY ISLAND introduced America's first roller coaster in 1884, and the completion of the subway in the 1920s transformed the island into a national playground for everyone to enjoy.

XOCHIMILCO's network of canals and floating gardens offers a glimpse into Mexico City's past and is best enjoyed by riding in trajineras (gondola-like boats).

BROOKLYN BRIDGE connects Manhattan and Brooklyn over the East River. When it opened in 1883, it was the longest suspension bridge ever built. New Yorkers doubted that it would actually hold, until P. T. Barnum proved them wrong when he marched his circus elephants across it.

COYOACÁN, whose name comes from the Nahuatl indigenous language and means "the place of coyotes," is an artistic and intellectual neighborhood of Mexico City. It has been home to many celebrated residents, including Frida Kahlo.

For Mom, Dad, and Mateo; with you, I am home

Copyright © 2019 by Tania de Regil. All rights reserved. No part of this book may be reproduced, transmitted, or stored in an information retrieval system in any form or by any means, graphic, electronic, or mechanical, including photocopying, taping, and recording, without prior written permission from the publisher. First edition 2019. Library of Congress Catalog Card Number pending. ISBN 978-1-5362-0193-2 (English hardcover). ISBN 978-1-5362-0675-3 (Spanish hardcover). This book was typeset in Hightower. The illustrations were done in ink, colored pencil, watercolor, and gouache and assembled digitally. Candlewick Press, 99 Dover Street, Somerville, Massachusetts 02144. visit us at www.candlewick.com.
Printed in Shenzhen, Guangdong, China. 19 20 21 22 23 24 CCP 10 9 8 7 6 5 4 3 2 1